GW01043771

About the Author

David Thompson was born and raised in Belfast, Northern Ireland. He always enjoyed writing poetry, but it wasn't until he became a dad that he decided to write children's books. David now lives with his wife, Emily, and their two children near Sevenoaks, Kent. *Daddy's Big Bike Race* is David's first attempt to make children smile through literature.

Daddy's Big Bike Race

David Thompson

Daddy's Big Bike Race

Olympia Publishers
London

www.olympiapublishers.com
OLYMPIA PAPERBACK EDITION

A CIP catalogue record for this title is
available from the British Library.

ISBN: 978-1-78830-174-9

First Published in 2019

Olympia Publishers
60 Cannon Street
London
EC4N 6NP

Printed in Great Britain

Dedication

Dedicated to three little angels:

Anna Lucy Mary Lewis
Grace Doran Moon
Vivienne Wren Williams

Acknowledgments

All the wonderful British cyclists who have inspired so many people, young and old, to get on their bikes. They have created a legacy for the next generation to follow in their tyre marks!

Dad's surprise party was finally here,
The house was filled with birthday cheer.
Streamers and paper chains hung overhead,
And his present was hidden outside in the shed.
As he came in the door Mum covered his eyes,
When he opened them up, we all shouted, "SURPRISE!"

After dancing and cake, Molly said with a grin,
"It's time to bring Daddy's present in."
As he unwrapped it, Charlie shrieked with delight,
"IT'S A SUPER DUPER RACING BIKE!
Willy Wighead rides one too
And I reckon he's as old as you!"

Dad straddled the saddle, it was quite a sight,
With his funny shaped glasses and pink shorts so tight.
His top was yellow, his helmet was green,
With lights front and back to make sure he'd be seen.

Then off he cycled at quite a pace.
When he came back he said, "I've entered a race.
I'm competing in London, I'll be on TV
So you can watch and cheer for me!"

LONDON – 2019

There was Dad and Wighead, McMoo and Broom.
They all lined up then the gun went BOOM.
Off they whizzed as quick as can be

Except for Dad who was drinking his tea.
It's not about speed, it's all about pace
That's the secret to winning this race.
Dad took a last gulp, put his cup on the tray,
Clipped his feet to the pedals and cycled away.

He rode out of the stadium, the road led him right.
Went up the first hill and sank out of sight
Dad sped down the hill with a wonderful swoosh,
Then suddenly he saw Wighead's head in a bush.
"Help, help," shouted Wighead, his face curled in a frown,
"I've lost my wig and I'm stuck upside down.

I was going too fast and my bike hit a stone
And into this twiggily bush I was thrown."
"Twiggily is right," Dad said, "Just look at your head.
Maybe we should all call you Twighead instead."
"Don't worry, Wighead, I'll soon get you out
If I can do it quickly we're still in with a shout."

So Dad turned Wighead round, put his feet on the ground
And fastened his wig that he'd only just found.
They got on their bikes and away they both flew.
Cycling was so much more fun with two.

Then up ahead they heard a loud thud.
McMoo had cycled straight into the mud.
They pulled alongside and Dad said with a shout,
"Give me your hand and I'll pull you out."

So McMoo reached out and Dad pulled him free,
Then McMoo said so appreciatively,
"Oh, thank you, Dad, I owe you one.
If you hadn't stopped, I'm not sure what I'd have done.
I would have been stuck there, stuck there all night,
But now the others are out of sight."

"Don't worry," said Dad, "It will all be fine,
It's a long way to the finish line.
It's not about speed, it's all about pace,
That's the secret to winning this race."

Off the three cycled as quick as they could.

The track led them into the gloomiest wood.
"It's so dark in here." "Nearly too dark to see,"
Said McMoo and Wighead respectively.
Dad calmly smiled, turned and said,
Whilst lifting his helmet from the top of his head,
"Don't worry, my helmet has lights front and back.
This will help keep us on the right track."

Dad switched the lights on and away they all sped.
Then suddenly there was a cry up ahead.
"Help me, I'm lost, I rode into a tree.
I've punctured both tyres and grazed my right knee."
Dad shone his light brightly into the gloom
and there by the tree sat the race leader, Broom.

"Don't worry, Broom, I've got just the thing,
That my two brilliant children insisted I bring.
A puncture repair kit and a first aid kit too.
We'll soon fix your knee and your bike good as new."
McMoo fixed the rear tyre and Wighead the front
And Dad bandaged Broom's knee that he'd hurt in the
shunt.

Then all four riders got back on their bikes.
Dad led the way because he had the lights.
They followed the track as fast as they could
And very soon they were out of the wood

Then up ahead they saw a sign.
Only one more mile to the finish line.
"Go for it, Dad," Broom said with a grin,
"Thanks for your help but it's your time to win."
Dad took a deep breath and picked up the pace,
And zoomed across the line to finish the race.

The Queen put a medal over Dad's head,
And with a smile looked up and said.
"Well done, Dad, I am pleased you won.
The race looked like a lot of fun
But more importantly for me, it was lovely to see
The way you helped the other three."

As the Queen sat back upon her throne
Dad thought to himself, it's time to go home.
He got back on his bike and waved to the crowd,
And they all waved back and cheered aloud.
He rode all the way home so quickly he sped
In time to tuck Molly and Charlie in bed.